Dinosa

MW00905873

Printed in the U.S.A. • ISBN: 1-40373-629-4 • 15998
08 09 10 11 12 NGS 10 9 8 7 6 5 4 3

Mesozoic Era

Millions of years ago, dinosaurs ruled the world! They lived during an era called the Mesozoic Era, which lasted from 245 to 65 million years ago (noted as mega-annum, or Ma).

The Mesozoic Era is divided into three time periods: the **Triassic** (245–208 Ma), the **Jurassic** (208–144 Ma), and the **Cretaceous** (144–65 Ma). Dinosaurs appeared on Earth toward the end of the Triassic Period.

> **Plateosaurus**
> *Flat lizard*
> ....
> **FAMILY:** Plateosaurids
> **PERIOD:** Late Triassic: 220 Ma
> **AREA:** France, Germany, Switzerland
> **LENGTH:** 20-26 feet
> **DIET:** leafy plants

The Triassic Period
245-208 million years ago

Plateosaurus

Plateosaurus was one of the first large dinosaurs and is also one of the best known. It probably fed on the foliage of very tall trees.

The Triassic Period
245-208 million years ago (Ma)

225 Ma	**220 Ma**	**Late Triassic**	**End of Triassic**
Coelophysis	*Plateosaurus*	*Melanosaurus*	*Fabrosaurus*

The Jurassic Period
208-144 Ma

194 Ma	**190-180 Ma**	**150 Ma**	**156-144 Ma**
Anchisaurus	*Dilophosaurus*	*Diplodocus*	*Ceratosaurus*

Herrerasaurus

Herrerasaurus is one of the earliest known dinosaurs. It probably fed on smaller dinosaurs or other reptiles.

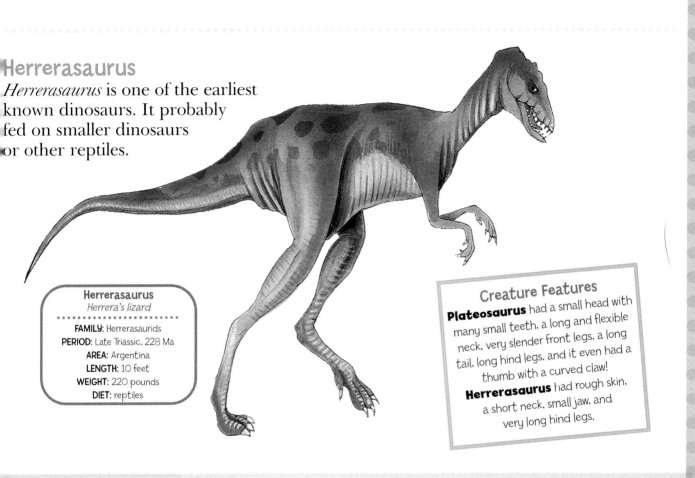

Herrerasaurus
Herrera's lizard

FAMILY: Herrerasaurids
PERIOD: Late Triassic, 228 Ma
AREA: Argentina
LENGTH: 10 feet
WEIGHT: 220 pounds
DIET: reptiles

Creature Features

Plateosaurus had a small head with many small teeth, a long and flexible neck, very slender front legs, a long tail, long hind legs, and it even had a thumb with a curved claw!

Herrerasaurus had rough skin, a short neck, small jaw, and very long hind legs.

The Cretaceous Period
144–65 Ma

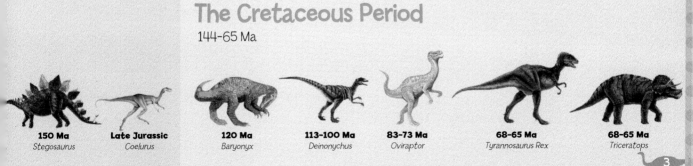

150 Ma
Stegosaurus

Late Jurassic
Coelurus

120 Ma
Baryonyx

113–100 Ma
Deinonychus

83–73 Ma
Oviraptor

68–65 Ma
Tyrannosaurus Rex

68–65 Ma
Triceratops

3

The Jurassic Period
208-144 million years ago

Stegosaurs (including *Kentrosaurus* shown here) were widespread during the late Jurassic Period. The first ornithopods and ankylosaurs also appeared, and the earliest birds joined the flying reptiles (pterosaurs) in the sky.

Yangchuanosaurus

Yangchuanosaurus was a bipedal (walking on two legs) carnivorous (meat-eating) dinosaur, with ridges and small hornlike bumps on its 3-foot-long head, and large jaws with long curved teeth.

Yangchuanosaurus
Yang-ch'uan lizard

FAMILY: Uncertain
PERIOD: Late Jurassic
AREA: China
LENGTH: 25 feet
DIET: carnivorous

Kentrosaurus
Spiked lizard

FAMILY: Stegosaurids
PERIOD: Late Jurassic: 156-150 Ma
AREA: Tanzania
LENGTH: 16.5 feet
DIET: low plants

The Cretaceous Period
144-65 million years ago

Triceratops

This species belonged to one of the last groups of quadrupedal (walking on four legs) herbivorous (plant-eating) dinosaurs. It reached 30 feet in length and may have weighed up to 10 tons.

Triceratops
Three-horned face

FAMILY: Ceratopsids
PERIOD: Late Cretaceous: 68–65 Ma
AREA: Canada, USA (Montana, North Dakota, South Dakota, Wyoming)
LENGTH: 30 feet **WEIGHT:** 8 tons
DIET: fibrous plants

Coelurosaurs

The coelurosaurs ("hollow-tailed lizards") were bipedal carnivores. Except for the king of all coelurosaurs—*Tyrannosaurus Rex*—they were all fairly small predators, being slender, lightly built and fast. They had small heads, narrow jaws with sharp teeth, long necks, and sharp claws. The coelurosaurs lived throughout the 165 million years in which the dinosaurs ruled the Earth.

Compsognathus

Although *Compsognathus* is one of the smallest known dinosaurs—about the size of a chicken—it was one of the fastest bipeds. Its hands had just two fingers. *Compsognathus* was easy prey for larger dinosaurs.

Compsognathus
Pretty jaw
- **FAMILY:** Compsognathids
- **PERIOD:** Late Jurassic: 156-150 Ma
- **AREA:** France, Germany (Bavaria)
- **LENGTH:** 2.5-4.5 feet
- **WEIGHT:** 6.5 pounds
- **DIET:** invertebrates, lizards

Coelurus
Hollow Tail
- **FAMILY:** Coelurids
- **PERIOD:** Late Jurassic
- **AREA:** USA (Wyoming)
- **LENGTH:** 6 feet
- **DIET:** small vertebrates

Coelurus

Coelurus had light, hollow bones and a small, flat head. It lived in North America and ran quickly on its two hind legs, hunting small dinosaurs, flying reptiles, and early mammals.

Creature Features

Compsognathus was compact and lightly built with a long tail to balance the body, long hind legs for running fast, a lightweight skull and delicate jaw.

Coelurus had a long, narrow head and jaws and sharp teeth, flexible neck, tough, coarse skin, and a very long tail.

Coelophysis
Hollow form
....

FAMILY: Coelophysids
PERIOD: 225 Ma
AREA: USA (Arizona, New Mexico)
LENGTH: 10 feet
WEIGHT: 60 pounds
DIET: small vertebrates

Tyrannosaurus Rex

This famous dinosaur has the reputation as a fierce and deadly predator. Fossils of *Tyrannosaurus* are very rare and scientists have had to reconstruct this huge dinosaur on the basis of a few bones and teeth.

Tyrannosaurus Rex
Tyrant lizard king
....

FAMILY: Tyrannosaurids
PERIOD: Late Cretaceous: 68–65 Ma
AREA: Canada, Asia, USA
LENGTH: 43 feet **WEIGHT:** 7.5 tons
DIET: herbivorous dinosaurs and carrion

Coelophysis

The name of this dinosaur means "hollow form." Many of the bones of its limbs were hollow. It is one of the earliest known dinosaurs.

What does it eat?
With a reputation as a fierce and deadly predator—the largest flesh-eating animal to have ever roamed the Earth—it's surprising to note that the T-Rex probably fed mainly on dead animals!

Toothless Theropods

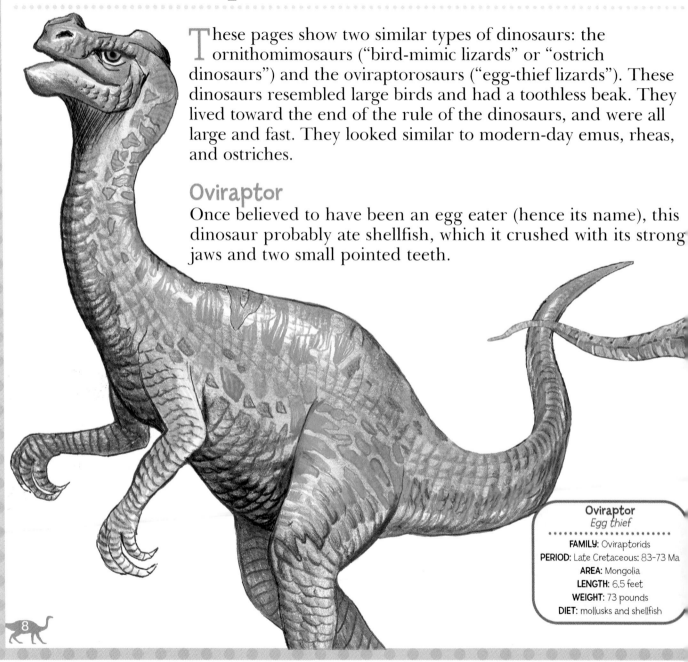

These pages show two similar types of dinosaurs: the ornithomimosaurs ("bird-mimic lizards" or "ostrich dinosaurs") and the oviraptorosaurs ("egg-thief lizards"). These dinosaurs resembled large birds and had a toothless beak. They lived toward the end of the rule of the dinosaurs, and were all large and fast. They looked similar to modern-day emus, rheas, and ostriches.

Oviraptor

Once believed to have been an egg eater (hence its name), this dinosaur probably ate shellfish, which it crushed with its strong jaws and two small pointed teeth.

Oviraptor
Egg thief

FAMILY: Oviraptorids
PERIOD: Late Cretaceous: 83-73 Ma
AREA: Mongolia
LENGTH: 6.5 feet
WEIGHT: 73 pounds
DIET: mollusks and shellfish

Gallimimus

This dinosaur had a thickset body, long thin legs, a slender neck, three-fingered hands, and a thin stiff tail.

Gallimimus
Chicken mimic
• • • • • • • • • • • • • •
FAMILY: Ornithomimids
PERIOD: Late Cretaceous: 73-65 Ma
AREA: Mongolia
LENGTH: 20 feet
DIET: small vertebrates, insects, plants

Struthiomimus
Ostrich mimic
• • • • • • • • • • • • • •
FAMILY: Ornithomimids
PERIOD: Late Cretaceous: 73-70 Ma
AREA: USA, Canada
LENGTH: 13 feet
WEIGHT: 330 pounds
DIET: small animals, plants

Creature Features

Gallimimus had a long and flexible neck, a very strong tail, and strong claws on its feet.

Struthiomimus had a beaked snout, short arms, strong claws, and a long tail to balance the body.

Struthiomimus

This dinosaur was very similar to the modern ostrich (*struthio* in Latin). It had small, drooping arms, a long tail, and dry scaly skin. It could run up to 50 miles per hour.

The First Carnosaurs

The name "carnosaurs" means "meat lizards." The typical carnosaur was large (over 20 feet long), bipedal, and heavily built, with powerful hind legs, much shorter front legs, and a large head set on a short muscular neck. These dinosaurs had a stiff, heavy tail that they used to balance their heavy bodies.

Dilophosaurus

This dinosaur had many fine teeth and a double-horned crest on its head. Its jaws were much smaller and weaker than those of other carnosaurs.

Allosaurus

This species probably ate medium-sized dinosaurs, such as *Ceratosaurus* or *Stegosaurus.*

Dilophosaurus
Two-crested lizard

FAMILY: Megalosaurids
PERIOD: Early Jurassic: 190–180 Ma
AREA: USA (Arizona), China
LENGTH: 20 feet
WEIGHT: 1100 pounds
DIET: herbivorous dinosaurs

Allosaurus
Alien lizard

FAMILY: Allosaurids
PERIOD: Late Jurassic, Early Cretaceous: 155–145 Ma
AREA: USA (Utah), Tanzania
LENGTH: 35 feet
WEIGHT: 1.5–2 tons
DIET: herbivorous dinosaurs

What does it eat?
These dinosaurs dined on their own—they ate other dinosaurs!

Ceratosaurus
Horned lizard

FAMILY: Ceratosaurids
PERIOD: Late Jurassic: 156-144 Ma
AREA: USA, Tanzania
LENGTH: 20-25 feet
WEIGHT: 1 ton (2,000 pounds)
DIET: herbivorous and aquatic dinosaurs

Megalosaurus
Great lizard

FAMILY: Megalosaurids
PERIOD: Middle Jurassic: 181-169 Ma
AREA: Great Britain
LENGTH: 30 feet
WEIGHT: 1 ton
DIET: herbivorous dinosaurs

Ceratosaurus

This dinosaur had a horn on its nose. Each hand had well-developed fingers.

Creature Feature
Megalosaurus was the first dinosaur to be scientifically described and named.

Megalosaurus

Megalosaurus had very powerful teeth, short front legs and long hind legs.

Cretaceous Carnosaurs

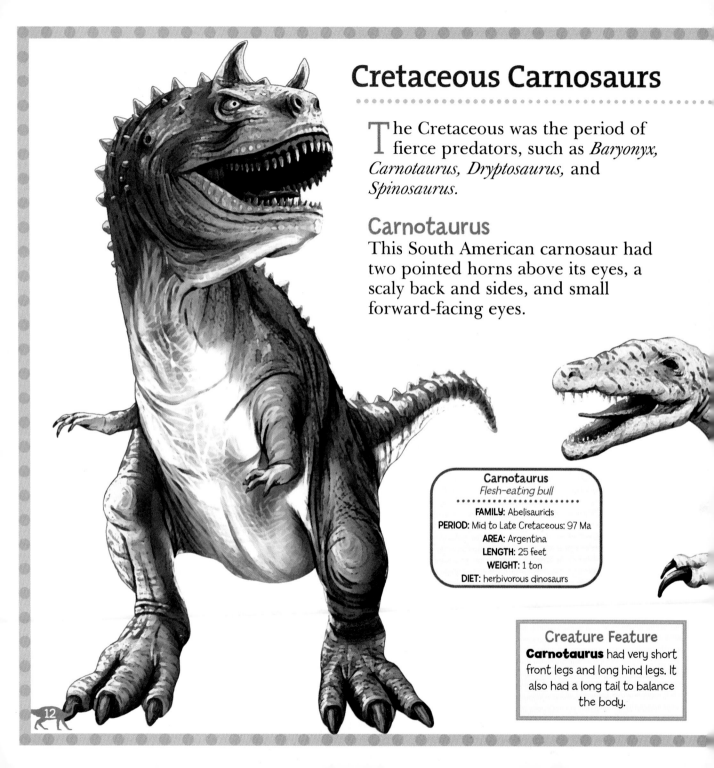

The Cretaceous was the period of fierce predators, such as *Baryonyx, Carnotaurus, Dryptosaurus,* and *Spinosaurus.*

Carnotaurus

This South American carnosaur had two pointed horns above its eyes, a scaly back and sides, and small forward-facing eyes.

Carnotaurus
Flesh-eating bull
. . . .
FAMILY: Abelisaurids
PERIOD: Mid to Late Cretaceous: 97 Ma
AREA: Argentina
LENGTH: 25 feet
WEIGHT: 1 ton
DIET: herbivorous dinosaurs

Creature Feature
Carnotaurus had very short front legs and long hind legs. It also had a long tail to balance the body.

Spinosaurus

Spinosaurus was the largest of all carnivorous dinosaurs. It had a "sail" up to 6 feet high running along its back.

Baryonyx
Heavy claw
. . . .
FAMILY: Baryonychids
PERIOD: Early to Mid Cretaceous: 120 Ma
AREA: Great Britain, Nigeria
LENGTH: 35 feet
WEIGHT: 2.2 tons
DIET: fish, carcasses

Spinosaurus
Spiny lizard
. . . .
FAMILY: Spinosaurids
PERIOD: Middle Cretaceous: 100-93 Ma
AREA: Egypt, Morocco, Tunisia
LENGTH: 50-55 feet
WEIGHT: 5-9 tons
DIET: fish, dinosaurs

Baryonyx

This dinosaur was discovered in 1983 and had a long, narrow jaw very similar to that of a crocodile.

Creature Feature
Baryonyx used its huge tail for defense.

Prosauropods

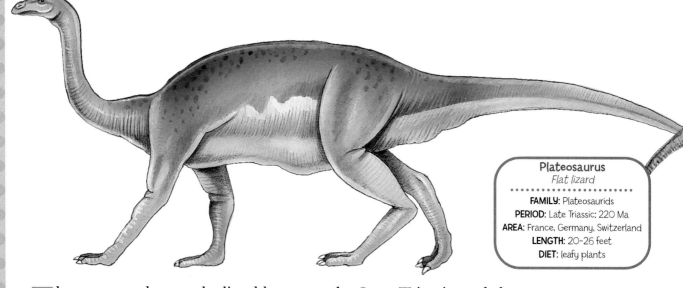

Plateosaurus
Flat lizard
....
FAMILY: Plateosaurids
PERIOD: Late Triassic: 220 Ma
AREA: France, Germany, Switzerland
LENGTH: 20-26 feet
DIET: leafy plants

The sauropodomorphs lived between the Late Triassic and the Early Jurassic. They can be divided into two infraorders: the prosauropods and the sauropods. The prosauropods ("before the sauropods") were the first group of herbivorous dinosaurs (until the Late Triassic almost all dinosaurs were carnivores), and among the first herbivores to feed on high foliage. The prosauropods varied in size, ranging from *Plateosaurus* (over 26 feet long) to the much smaller *Anchisaurus* (up to 8 feet long).

Plateosaurus

Along with *Melanorosaurus, Plateosaurus* was one of the largest prosauropods, growing up to 26 feet long. It is thought to have been a quadruped, standing on its powerful hind legs only to browse the leaves of tall trees. *Plateosaurus* had a small head and a fairly short neck.

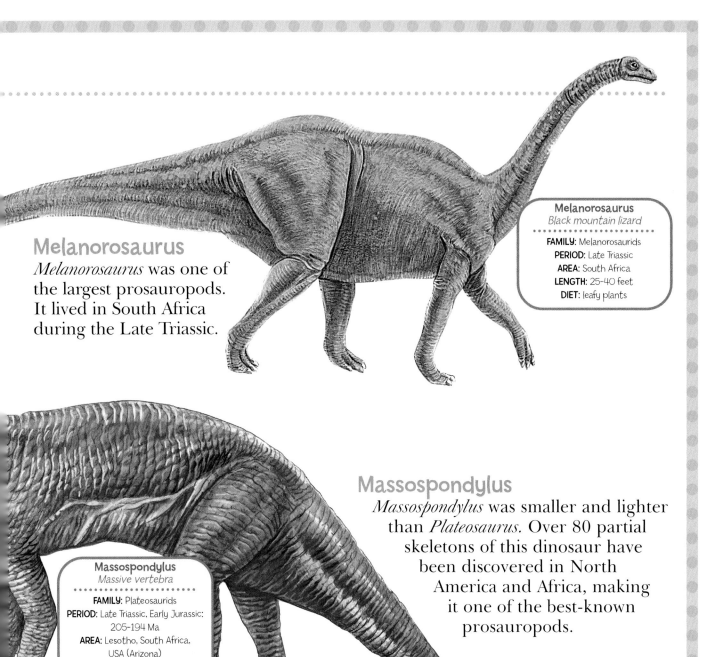

Melanorosaurus

Melanorosaurus was one of the largest prosauropods. It lived in South Africa during the Late Triassic.

Melanorosaurus
Black mountain lizard
. . . .
FAMILY: Melanorosaurids
PERIOD: Late Triassic
AREA: South Africa
LENGTH: 25–40 feet
DIET: leafy plants

Massospondylus

Massospondylus was smaller and lighter than *Plateosaurus.* Over 80 partial skeletons of this dinosaur have been discovered in North America and Africa, making it one of the best-known prosauropods.

Massospondylus
Massive vertebra
. . . .
FAMILY: Plateosaurids
PERIOD: Late Triassic, Early Jurassic: 205–194 Ma
AREA: Lesotho, South Africa, USA (Arizona)
LENGTH: 16.5 feet
DIET: leafy plants

Sauropods

The sauropods ("lizard feet") survived for around 140 million years, from the beginning of the Jurassic until the end of the Cretaceous, spreading all over the world. They ranged from large to gigantic!

Diplodocus
Double beam
. . . .
FAMILY: Diplodocids
PERIOD: Late Jurassic: 150 Ma
AREA: USA (Colorado, Utah, Wyoming)
LENGTH: 89 feet
WEIGHT: 15 tons
DIET: leaves, ferns

Diplodocus
Diplodocus was lighter than most sauropods (it weighed only 11–17 tons). However, large specimens could reach almost 100 feet long with their tail fully outstretched.

Mamenchisaurus
Mamenchisaurus had the longest neck of all known animals, which could grow up to 50 feet, with 19 vertebrae. This herbivore probably lived in herds to protect itself from carnosaur predators.

Shunosaurus

Shunosaurus had a club-shaped tail with two pairs of short spikes. Many skeletons of this sauropod have been discovered, making it one of the best-known dinosaurs.

Shunosaurus
Shu lizard

FAMILY: Cetiosaurids
PERIOD: Middle Jurassic
AREA: China
LENGTH: 33 feet
WEIGHT: 2.75 tons
DIET: leaves

Mamenchisaurus
Mamenchi lizard

FAMILY: Euhelopodids
PERIOD: Late Jurassic: 145-160 Ma
AREA: China
LENGTH: 70-90 feet
WEIGHT: 28.5 tons
DIET: leaves

Creature Feature
Brachiosaurus was one of the largest land animals to ever roam the Earth.

Brachiosaurus
Arm lizard

FAMILY: Brachiosaurids
PERIOD: 153-113 Ma
AREA: Algeria, Portugal, Tanzania, USA (Colorado, Utah, Wyoming)
LENGTH: 82 feet
WEIGHT: 45-55 tons
DIET: conifers, cycads, ferns

Iguanodontids

The iguanodontid dinosaurs ranged from medium to large. They lived between the Late Jurassic and Late Cretaceous, all over the world. The iguanodontids had a large skull with a long snout ending in a toothless beak, used for grazing and browsing. These massive animals had sturdy hind legs to support their weight. Their first fingers ("thumbs") had a strong spike that they probably used as a weapon if attacked. The iguanodontids carried their stiff, heavy tails outstretched and raised to balance their bodies. One of the best known is *Iguanodon*.

Iguanodon
Iguana tooth
· ·
FAMILY: Iguanodontids
PERIOD: Early to Middle
Cretaceous: 140-110 Ma
AREA: Great Britain, Mongolia, USA
LENGTH: 30-40 feet
WEIGHT: 3-5 tons
DIET: plants

Deinonychosaurs

The deinonychosaurs had a vicious sicklelike claw on the second toe of each foot. In fact, the name *Deinonychus* means "terrible claw." Although lightly built and relatively small, these dinosaurs were extraordinary predators, hunting small reptiles and mammals alone and in packs. The best known is *Velociraptor*.

Velociraptor
Swift thief
· ·
FAMILY: Dromaeosaurids
PERIOD: Late Cretaceous: 83-70 Ma
AREA: China, Mongolia
LENGTH with tail: 6 feet
DIET: herbivorous dinosaurs

Hadrosaurs

Hadrosaurs are also known as "duckbilled dinosaurs," due to their wide, flat beaks. The first hadrosaurs appeared during the Middle Cretaceous and died out 30 million years later, along with all the other dinosaurs. The best known is *Hadrosaurus*.

Hadrosaurus
Bulky lizard
. . . .
FAMILY: Hadrosaurids
PERIOD: Late Cretaceous: 80 Ma
AREA: Canada, USA (Montana, New Jersey, New Mexico, South Dakota)
LENGTH: 25–33 feet
DIET: plants

Pachycephalosaurs

The pachycephalosaurs ("thick-headed lizards") were bipedal herbivores that lived between the Late Jurassic and Late Cretaceous. They had a very thick skull, often adorned with "knobs" or spikes; large, sturdy bodies; short front legs; and a long, stiff tail. *Pachycephalosaurus* was the largest dinosaur of the group, reaching up to 15 feet in length and with a 10-inch-thick domed skull.

Pachycephalosaurus
Thick-headed lizard
. . . .
FAMILY: Pachycephalosaurids
PERIOD: Late Cretaceous: 68–65 Ma
AREA: USA (Montana, South Dakota, Wyoming)
LENGTH: 16 feet
DIET: plants, insects

Lambeosaurs

These "duckbilled" dinosaurs lived in herds and bred in colonies, probably for safety reasons. Many had large hollow crests on top of their heads. Some scientists believe that lambeosaurids communicated with each other by making trumpeting noises through their crests.

Corythosaurus
Helmet lizard
....
FAMILY: Lambeosaurids
PERIOD: Late Cretaceous: 75 Ma
AREA: Canada, USA
LENGTH: 33 feet **WEIGHT:** 4.2 tons
DIET: plants

Parasaurolophus
Like Saurolophus
....
FAMILY: Lambeosaurids
PERIOD: Late Cretaceous: 76–73 Ma
AREA: North America
LENGTH: 33 feet
DIET: plants

Stegosaurs

The stegosaurs were herbivores that lived from the Jurassic to the Cretaceous and spread over Europe, Asia, North America, and Africa. They were medium to large in size, with strong, thick legs, massive bodies, two rows of plates or bony spikes along the back, and at least two pairs of tail spikes. These slow-moving animals used their tail spikes as lethal weapons to defend themselves from predators. The back plates may have helped to regulate the dinosaur's body temperature. Stegosaurs had tiny heads and brains.

Stegosaurus
Roof lizard

FAMILY: Stegosaurids
PERIOD: Late Jurassic: 150 Ma
AREA: Europe, USA (Colorado, Utah, Wyoming)
LENGTH: 30 feet
WEIGHT: 2-5 tons
DIET: low plants

Tuojiangosaurus
Tuo river lizard

FAMILY: Stegosaurids
PERIOD: Late Jurassic: 156 Ma
AREA: China
LENGTH: 23 feet
DIET: low plants

Ceratopsians

The ceratopsians ("horned faces") were herbivores that inhabited Asia and North America during the Cretaceous Period. Many had a bony neck frill and horns on their snout or head. The earlier protoceratopsids had a neck frill, but no horns.

The ceratopsians' nests were sandy mounds, measuring 6.5 feet across and 3 feet deep, which the females made with their snouts or feet. They normally contained about 20 eggs, which were partially buried to protect them from the outside temperature.

Protoceratops

Protoceratops was one of the smallest horned dinosaurs and had a parrot-like beak to sever grass stems, and teeth like scissors to chop them.

Protoceratops
First horned face
. . . .
FAMILY: Protoceratopsids
PERIOD: Late Cretaceous: 85-78 Ma
AREA: China, Mongolia
LENGTH: 6 feet
WEIGHT: 400 pounds
DIET: fibrous plants

Triceratops

Triceratops, the largest known ceratopsian, weighed about the same as an elephant.

Triceratops
Three-horned face
. . . .
FAMILY: Ceratopsids
PERIOD: Late Cretaceous: 68-65 Ma
AREA: Canada, USA (Montana, North Dakota, South Dakota, Wyoming)
LENGTH: 26-30 feet
WEIGHT: 6-12 tons
DIET: fibrous plants

Styracosaurus
Spiked lizard
. . . .
FAMILY: Ceratopsids
PERIOD: Late Cretaceous: 75-72 Ma
AREA: Canada, USA (Montana)
LENGTH: 18 feet
WEIGHT: 3 tons
DIET: fibrous plants

Styracosaurus

Styracosaurus had a nose horn and a neck frill with six long spikes around the edge.

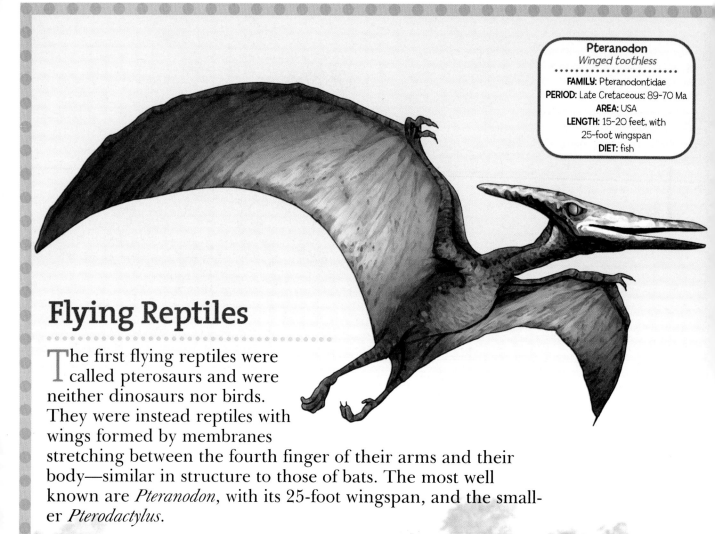

Flying Reptiles

The first flying reptiles were called pterosaurs and were neither dinosaurs nor birds. They were instead reptiles with wings formed by membranes stretching between the fourth finger of their arms and their body—similar in structure to those of bats. The most well known are *Pteranodon*, with its 25-foot wingspan, and the smaller *Pterodactylus*.

Pteranodon

Pteranodon was a flying reptile, closely related to dinosaurs. It had a toothless beak like a modern bird, but is believed to have been quadrupedal, walking on all four limbs, unlike a bird. Its wing shape suggests that it flew somewhat like an albatross, soaring aloft, particularly over open waters in search of fish.